Blessed Longing

A poetic guidebook through the

"vast and open world"

of Johann Wolfgang Goethe

-English renderings by Keith Stanton
-Illustrations by Tim Joyce

Order this book online at www.trafford.com/08-0084
or email orders@trafford.com

Most Trafford titles are also available at major online book retailers.

Illustrator: Tim Joyce

Editor: Emily Bunker

Cover Artwork: Tim Joyce

Designer: Keith Stanton

Note for Librarians: A cataloguing record for this book is available from Library
and Archives Canada at www.collectionscanada.ca/amicus/index-e.html

Printed in Victoria, BC, Canada.

ISBN: 978-1-4251-6922-0

*We at Trafford believe that it is the responsibility of us all, as both individuals
and corporations, to make choices that are environmentally and socially sound.
You, in turn, are supporting this responsible conduct each time you purchase a
Trafford book, or make use of our publishing services. To find out how you are
helping, please visit www.trafford.com/responsiblepublishing.html*

*Our mission is to efficiently provide the world's finest, most comprehensive
book publishing service, enabling every author to experience success.
To find out how to publish your book, your way, and have it available
worldwide, visit us online at www.trafford.com/10510*

Trafford
PUBLISHING™ www.trafford.com

North America & international
toll-free: 1 888 232 4444 (USA & Canada)
phone: 250 383 6864 ♦ fax: 250 383 6804 ♦ email: info@trafford.com

The United Kingdom & Europe
phone: +44 (0)1865 487 395 ♦ local rate: 0845 230 9601
facsimile: +44 (0)1865 481 507 ♦ email: info.uk@trafford.com

10 9 8 7 6 5 4

FOREWORD

Goethe is widely regarded not only as the foremost literary figure in the German language, but as an icon of World Literature (a concept we, in fact, owe to him), one who can be placed on a level with Homer, Dante and Shakespeare. Unfortunately, his greatness is not easily accessible to readers lacking knowledge of German. In his long life (1749–1832), Goethe never ceased to develop. Indeed, this dynamic of constant growth is an essential feature of his writing. Consequently, the true nature of his genius is best apprehended through a variety of works from different stages of his development. Not surprisingly, the purest and most traceable manifestation of Goethe's metamorphosis is to be found in his lyric poems. These, however, depend the most for their effect on his successful manipulation of his mother tongue and, hence, stand to lose the most in translation.

One need only examine the German words for "poet" (Dichter), "poem" (Gedicht) and "poetry" (Dichtung) to see how far removed from our own notion of this elusive art the German concept is. Our English terms all derive from the Greek "poiein" (to make). The invention of elaborate imagery and figurative elements on which much English poetry (including Shakespeare's) depends reflects this basic understanding of poetry as a process of "making" something new and wondrous. In contrast, the equivalent German words all share the root "dicht" (meaning "dense"). To the German mind, the poet is one who condenses experience, making it more powerfully concentrated. (See Walter Kaufmann's introduction to his *Twenty German Poets*, Copyright 1962 by Random House.) Some of Goethe's finest poems (such as the second "Wanderer's Night Song") are remarkable for the brevity and directness with which they convey layers of meaning.

If much, though certainly not all, of the best German verse dispenses with extensive imagery and figures, what makes it "poetic"? The answer, suggested above, could only be: a fresh and skillful use of the potential strengths of the German language itself; but in what ways important for the creation of poetry does German differ from English?

First of all, German possesses a wealth of sonorous vowel sounds which are articulated with greater purity and precision than in English. (One need only compare the pronunciation of the German "geht" with the English "gate".) Consonants, too, are given a more definitive "attack" (to borrow a musical expression). The combination of these two qualities gives a stronger identity or "value" to German syllables, in contrast to the frequent vagueness of their English counterparts. By capitalizing on these inherent properties, a gifted poet can make the counterpoint of meter and rhythm a truly musical force.

German word order, too, is more flexible than that of English. This feature enables a poet to give particular words a singular weight and magic, simply by their strategic placement. In the following translations every effort was made to respect these word positions, provided the result did not prove too unnatural in English.

The third and perhaps most important difference between the two languages lies in the greater homogeneity of German. English has gone through many, sometimes violent shifts of development (such as the one following the Norman Conquest). Present day English is only 20 to 25% Anglo-Saxon. Many of our everyday words, to which we have a more familiar, intimate connection (like "father", "mother", "earth" and "sun") have this Germanic basis. Most of our more complex words, however, are composed of roots from foreign tongues which we can only know through deliberate study. In German, on the other hand, the most abstract word generally is made up of smaller German words which have accompanied German-speakers since childhood and to which they can relate in an immediate, existential way. This means, of course, that a poet can probe the ineffable with language that never loses the vivid concreteness of fruit hanging ripe on a tree. It also explains why the best German verse is only subtly different from natural speech.

Indeed, Goethe felt an aversion to the written word. To him, consigning language to the permanence of dead parchment meant tearing it out of the living web of experience that gave it birth. Whenever possible, he preferred to dictate his poems to a secretary. For similar reasons, he never actually composed in an intricate meter (such as the elegiac distich of the "Roman Elegies", "Venetian Epigrams" and "Euphrosyne") until he had carried its pattern within him long enough to employ it spontaneously.

Most of the poems in this collection originally rhymed. While attempting to preserve the meter and at times the rhythm of Goethe's verse, I have rejected the use of rhyme for these English renderings. Even the best rhymed translations can sound contrived, and do the greatest disservice to a poet who strove for naturalness. The more flexible devices of consonance, assonance and alliteration will, I hope, restore some of the original harmony while doing less damage to the sense and sensibility of the original.

I had originally intended to divide this little book into chapters reflecting Goethe's universally acknowledged creative periods. Then I realized that such an arrangement would destroy the sense of organic continuity that so distinguishes Goethe. Suffice it to mention that the poems are presented in a general chronological order, with some deviations within periods for the sake of contrast, unity or "soul narration". The selection begins with Goethe's Sturm und Drang phase, follows the shift toward philosophical introspection in his early Weimar years, samples the more intimate monuments of his classical style, lingers long and with obvious preference on his competitive "dialogue" with the Persian poet Hafiz, to end with a glimpse into the rarified, higher visions of the Old Olympian.

My deepest thanks to Tim Joyce, not only for the superb illustrations, but for his invaluable feedback and suggestions. I am also indebted to Emily Bunker for her indispensible technical assistance.

K.S., January 22, 2008

For my parents

(Short "private" lyrics from letters to Friederike Brion)

Do I love you? I don't know.
If I look just once upon your face,
Look just once into your eyes,
My heart is freed from all its pain.
God knows, how I can be so blessed!
Do I love you? I don't know.

*

I'm coming soon, you golden children,
In vain does winter shut us in
Within our rooms so safe and warm.
We will sit down by the fire,
Delight ourselves a thousand ways,
And love just like the angels do.
We will wind our little wreaths,
We will bind our flowers in bunches
And do what little children do.

*

Now the angel feels what I feel,
At play I won her heart to me
And now her heart's completely mine.
You gave this joy to me, oh fate,
Now let each new day be like this one
And teach me to be worthy of her.

*

Oh, how much I long for you,
Little angel, just in dreams,
Just in dreams appear to me!
Though within them I might suffer,
Struggling anxiously for you with spirits,
Waking up all out of breath;
Oh, how much I long for you,
Oh, how dear you are to me,
Even in a troubling dream.

On a Painted Ribbon

Tiny flowers, tiny leaves
Are strewn for me, with playful hand,
By friendly, youthful gods of spring,
Upon a ribbon- light as air.

West wind, take it on your wing,
Slip it round my darling's dress!
So she steps before the mirror,
All in her bright liveliness.

Sees the roses wrapped around her,
Sees herself, a rose so young:
Just one look, beloved life!
And I have my full reward.

Feel what this heart is feeling,
Freely give your hand to me,
And may the bond that binds us
Be not fragile, like some rosy band!

Welcome and Parting

My heart was pounding- mount and gallop!
It was no sooner thought than done.
The evening rocked the earth to sleep,
And on the mountains hung the night;
The oak stood wrapped in cloaks of mist,
A towering giant looming there,
Where darkness from the bushes peered
With hundreds of black hollow eyes.

The moon upon that clouded hill
Shone through the haze so sadly pale,
The breezes flapped their quiet wings,
And brushed my ear with ghostly whirring.
The night produced a thousand phantoms,
But fresh and cheerful was my mood:
What fire I felt within my veins!
And in my heart, what glowing warmth!

I saw you, and the sweetest joy
Flowed from those gracious eyes to me.
Full was my heart as I sat near you
And drew my every breath for you.
A rosy colored vernal weather
Lit up that lovely face of yours,
And tenderness- for me? Oh God!
I'd hoped for it, without deserving.

But oh! With that first morning sun
The word "goodbye" constricts my heart:
In every kiss of yours, what bliss!
And in your look, what awful pain!
I left- you stood and lowered your head,
Then watched me leave, with watery eyes:
And yet, what joy, to know I'm loved!
And loving someone, God, what joy!

Wake up, oh Friederike,
Drive off the night,
Which just one look of yours
Can change to day.
The birds, in gentle whispers,
Call full of love
For my beloved sisters
To finally wake.

Is your word not sacred?
My peace of soul?
Wake up, oh heartless one!
You slumber still!
Hear- Philomel's lament
Is mute today,
Because that wicked sleep
Won't let you be.

The morning's shimmer trembles
With timid light
That blushes through your room,
But doesn't wake you.
At your sister's breast,
That heaves for you,
You fall asleep more deeply,
The more dawn breaks.

I see you sleeping, fair one,
    And from my eye
A tear wells up and falls
    And makes me blind.
Who could watch unfeeling?
    Who not burn up?
Though he were made of ice
    From head to toe!

Perhaps in dreams, dear joy!
    You see my shade,
Which half-asleep berates
    His muse in rhymes.
See how his face by turns
    Grows red and pale:
    Sleep has left him,
    Yet he's not awake.

While sleeping you have missed
    The nightingale,
As punishment now hear
    The words I've rhymed.
The verses weighed me down,
    Like a heavy yoke:
The fairest of my muses,
    You– were still asleep.

May Celebration

In what glorious light
Nature shines for me!
The sun, how it gleams
On the laughing meadow!

There are buds pushing forth
From every branch,
And a thousand voices
From every bush,

And joy's vibration
From every breast.
Oh earth and sun,
Oh blissful heart,

Oh power of love
So golden fair,
Like morning clouds up
Upon those hills,

You bless in glory
The fresh, green field,
In a mist of blossoms
The full, rich world!

Girl, sweet girl,
I love you so!
And your eyes are saying
You love me too.

Just as the lark
Loves its song and air,
And morning flowers
The scent of heaven,

So do I love you
With glowing blood,
You who've given me courage
And youth and joy

To dance new dances
And sing new songs-
May you ever be happy,
As you are in your love.

A tender youthful melancholy
Drives me to barren fields:
In a quiet morning slumber
Lies our mother earth. You hear
An icy wind that rocks the frozen boughs
And sings a chilling music to my song of pain,
And nature seems so anxious, still and mournful,
And yet more hopeful than my heart.
For see, it won't be long, oh sun god, till
That pair of twins, with soft blue eyes and curly
Golden hair, a rose wreath in their rounded hands,
Comes fluttering toward you on your path. And to dance
On newborn meadows see
That young man go, his hat
Adorned with ribbons, while the girl is picking
Violets from the budding grass, and bending down
She checks her breasts in secret, with joy she sees
Them fuller now and more inviting than they
Bloomed a year ago on Maypole day;
And feels and hopes.
God bless for me that man there
Working in his garden! How timely he begins
To loosen up the soil for seeding!
March has barely torn the cloak
Of snow from Winter's haggard flanks,
Who fled in storm and on the land has cast
A veil of mist, which hides the river, fields
And hills in frigid gray.
There he walks without delay,
His soul so full of harvest dreams,
And sows and hopes.

Wanderer's Storm Song

The one you won't abandon, spirit,
Neither rain nor storm can breathe
A shudder of fear upon his heart.
The one you won't abandon, spirit,
Greets the rain cloud,
Greets the hail storm,
With his singing,
Like the skylark,
You above.

The one you don't abandon, spirit,
You will lift above the mud-path
With your wings of fire.
He will walk
With flowers for feet
Upon Deucalion's mud-flows,
Python-slaying, light, huge,
Pythian Apollo.

The one you don't abandon, spirit,
Under him you'll spread your woolly wings
When he sleeps upon the rocks,
Drape him with protective pinions
In the grove when midnight comes.

The one you won't abandon, spirit,
You will snugly wrap in warmth
When the flurry strikes.
Drawn in by the warmth come muses,
Drawn by warmth those lovely graces.

Hover round me,
Muses, graces!
That is water, that is earth,
And the son of water and of earth
Over which I wander
Like a god.

You are pure like the heart of water,
You are pure as the marrow of earth,
You hover round me and I hover
Over water, over earth,
Like a god.

Should he make it home,
That little, swarthy, fiery peasant!
He make it home, expecting only
Your gifts, father Bromius,
And bright, glowing, warm encircling fire,
He keep his courage?
While I, with whom you walk,
Muses and graces all,
Whom all things await
That muses and graces
Bestow on life as a glorious wreath,
I walk discouraged?

Father Bromius,
You're the spirit,
Century's spirit,
Are what inner warmth
Was to Pindar,
What Phoebus Apollo
Is to the world.

No! No! Inner warmth!
Warmth of soul,
Find your center!
Project your glow toward
Phoebus Apollo,
Otherwise his princely gaze,
Turning cold,
Might pass you by,
Struck by envy,
Linger on the cedars' strength,
Which bear their green
Without his help.

But why does my song name you last,
You, with whom it started,
You, in whom it ends,
You, from whom it springs,
Jupiter Pluvius?
A Castalian fountain
Runs for indolent
Fortunate mortals
Off to your side,
You whose firm grasp covers me now,
Jupiter Pluvius.

Not by the elm
Have you visited him
With that pair of doves
In his cradling hands,
Crowned with a wreath of friendly roses,
Not Anacreon,
Storm-breathing god!

Nor in a forest of poplars
On the shores of Sybaris,
On the mountaintop's sunlit forehead,
Have you visited him,
The beelike singing,
Honey-babbling,
Friendly waving
Theocritus.

When chariots rattled
Wheel upon wheel, fast by the finish,
The cracking whips
Of victory-hot youth
Flew up high,
As dust rolled down
From mountain to valley,
A storm of gravel,
Your soul then glowed at danger, Pindar,
With courage. Glowed?
Pitiful heart,
Heavenly power,
Just enough warmth
To arrive at my hut,
Trudge to my goal.

Prometheus

Cover up your heavens, Zeus,
With murk and cloud!
And practice, like a
Thistle-chopping boy,
On lofty oaks and mountain peaks!
My earth, however,
You must leave standing,
Likewise my hut,
Which you did not construct,
And my hearth's fire,
The warmth of which
You envy me.

I know of nothing sorrier
Under the sun than you gods!
How pitifully you feed
Your majesty
On tithes of victims
And the breath of prayer,
And would starve, were not
Children and beggars
Dupes of empty hope.

Once, as a child,
Finding no home, no exit,
I turned my erring eye
Toward the sun, as if there I'd find
An ear, ready to hear my cry,
A heart like mine
To pity my affliction.

Who helped me fight the
Haughtiness of Titans?
Who rescued me from slavery,
From death?
Did you not do it all yourself,
Holy, glowing heart?
And, betrayed by youthful goodness,
Glow with thanks for rescue
To that sleeper up above?

I honor you? What for?
Have you once lessened the pain
Of those who were burdened?
Have you ever dried the tears
Of those who were anxious?
Was I not forged into a man
By almighty time
And fate eternal,
Both your lords and mine?

Perhaps you supposed
That I should hate this life,
Flee into a wasteland,
Just because some dream-buds of
Youth's morning failed to ripen?

Here I sit, forming men
In my own image,
A race designed to be like me,
To suffer, weep,
Rejoice and take enjoyment,
And hold you, as I do-
In scorn!

Ganymede

How in dawn's red light
You glow all around me,
Spring, dear companion!
With a thousand times the bliss of love
That sacred sense
Of your heavenly warmth
Presses against my heart,
You infinite beauty!

Could I but clasp you, girl,
In these arms!

Ah, upon your breast
I lie and languish,
And your flowers, your grass,
Press themselves to my heart.
You cool the fiery
Thirst of my own breast,
Sweet lovely morning wind.
Lovingly the nightingale
Calls to me from the misty vale.

I'm here! I'm coming!
Where to, though, where to?

Straight up! That's where I'm drawn!
The clouds, they are floating
Downward, they fall to
Meet halfway the force of my love,
To me, me!
Within your lap
Upward,
Embracing embraced!
Upward
Against your bosom,
You all-loving Father!

Mohammed's Song

See the rocky spring,
Bright as joy,
Like a glowing star!
Over clouds
His childhood has been nourished
By kindly spirits
In bushes between cliffs.

Fresh as youth
He dances from the cloud
Down upon that shelf of marble,
Splashing joy back
To the sky.

Through summit paths
He chases motley stones,
And with early leader's step
He tears his brother springs
Along with him.

Down below beneath his steps
Flowers spring forth throughout the valley,
And the meadow
Lives upon his breath.

But no shady vale can hold him,
Nor the flowers
Which, wrapped around his knees,
Seek to coax him with their loving eyes;
Toward the plain he's driven on his course,
Serpentine.

Brooks then press against him,
Seeking friendship.
Now he steps
Into the plain in silver splendor,
And the valley sparkles with him,
And the rivers from the plains
And the brooks that leave the mountains
Cheer him on and cry out: Brother!
Brother, take your brothers with you,
Down to your primeval father,
To the ocean that's eternal,
Who with outstretched arms is waiting
For us all,
Which, alas, reach out in vain
To clasp all those who long for him;
For the hungry desert sand
Devours us,
The sun above, it
Sucks away our blood,
A hill can
Shut us into ponds.
Brother,
Take your brothers from the plains,
Take your brothers from the mountains
With you, to your father, with you!

Come ye all!
And now he swells
More gloriously, an entire race
Lifts the prince upon its back,
And in a roll of triumph he
Gives names to all the lands, as cities
Too emerge beneath his feet.

Inexorably he rushes onward,
Leaves the flaming peaks of towers,
Marble houses, offspring of
His fullness, in his wake.

Cedar houses Atlas carries
On his giant shoulders, while
Above his head a thousand sails
Waft his power and glory
Upward to the sky.

And thus he carries all his brothers,
All his treasures, all his children
To the waiting, primal maker,
To break upon his heart with joy.

To Coachman Kronos

Speed it up Kronos!
On with that rattling trot!
Downhill glides our path;
Dizzying nausea stews in my
Head as you tarry!
Fresh now the bumpy trot
Over sticks, roots and stones,
Swiftly- straight into life!

Now once again
The slow breathing pace,
Strenuously plodding uphill.
Up now, you snail!
Onward you strive and you hope.

Wide, high, glorious the view
From all sides deep into life,
From peak to high peak
The infinite spirit
Pregnant with life without end.

To the side the shade of the shelter
Now draws you,
The girl standing there at the threshold,
Eyes that promise refreshment.
Sip deep! For me, girl,
This draught frothing over,
That friendly look wishing me health.

Down now, more freshly down!
See the sun sinking.
Before it does set, before in some moor
A fog knocks me down in old age,
My toothless jaw chattering,
Bones hanging shaking and loose,

Then rip me away,
Drunk from that ray,
A fiery sea in my foaming
Eye, blinded and tumbling,
Off to that nightly portal of hell.

Coachman, blow on your horn,
Let the rattling canter resound,
Let Orcus know, a prince is approaching,
That the mighty might rise from their seats.

The King of Thule

There was a king in Thule,
So faithful to the grave,
To whom his love, while dying,
Gave a cup of gold.

It was his prized possession,
He drained it at each feast,
Tears would flood his eyes
Whenever he would drink.

And when his time had come,
He counted realms and towns,
Gave all things to his heirs,
But not the cherished cup.

He sat at the king's banquet,
The knights surrounding him,
In that high ancestral hall
In the castle by the sea.

The aging drinker stood there,
And drank life's final glow,
Then cast the sacred goblet
To the element below.

He watched it fall and fill
With water till it sank,
His eyes would soon be closing,
He never drank again.

New Love, New Life

Heart, my heart, what's all this reeling,
  What oppresses you so much?
What a strange new life I'm feeling-
  I don't know you any more.
Gone is everything you once loved,
Gone is all that made you gloomy,
Gone your effort and your rest-
Oh, what brought you to this state?

Does this flower of youth enchain you,
  This delightful, lovely form?
These benevolent, faithful eyes
  With uncanny, infinite force?
If I pull away in haste,
To gather courage and escape her,
  At that very moment I am
Led right back into her sphere.

And upon this magic thread,
  Which will not let itself be cut,
That dear wanton maiden holds me
  Fast, so much against my will.
Now I'm forced to live within her
Magic circle, as she chooses;
What a change this is, how great!
Love, oh love, please let me go!

To Belinda

Why do you pull me, so I can't resist,
Into that garish world?
Wasn't I good-hearted, young and happy,
In the barren night?

Tucked away within my tiny room,
I lay in moon's soft glow;
Its trembling radiance wrapped itself around me,
As my senses dimmed.

I dreamed back then of full and golden hours
Of untainted joy;
Already felt your image with foreboding,
Deep within my breast.

Is this me, whom at the gaming table
You tie with all those lights?
Often seating me across from faces
That I cannot stand?

The lovely bloom of spring upon the fields
Has lost its charm for me;
Where you are, angel, there is love and goodness,
Nature's now- with you.

Longing

This tear won't be the last to well
Up burning from the heart,
And with unspeakable new pain
Give birth to pain by drying.

May I always, here and there,
Feel eternal love,
Though pain, too, keep on burrowing
Through every vein and nerve.

Could I but be completely filled
By you, eternal spirit!
This deep and chronic torment,
How long it lasts on earth!

In Autumn 1775

Thicken greener, oh leaves,
On this vine trellis here,
That runs right up to my window.
Swell, press together,
Berry clusters, and ripen
Faster to glistening fullness.
You're incubated by the parting gaze
Of the mother sun, and caressed
By the fruitful fullness
Of loving sky.
You're cooled by the friendly magic
Breath of the moon,
And watered, alas,
From these eyes,
By the full swelling tears
Of eternally life-giving love.

On the Lake

I suck new blood, new nourishment
From a vast and open world.
How good and giving nature is,
Which holds me to its breast.
Each wavelet rocks our small boat on
In rhythm with the oars,
And mountains piercing clouds and sky
Are here to meet our course.

Eyes, why do you lower yourselves?
Golden dreams, are you returning?
Dream- be gone, however golden!
Love and life are here as well.

On the waves are sparkling
Thousands of floating stars.
From every side a soft mist drinks
The towering distance.
Morning breezes wing around
The shadowy inlet,
And upon the lake is mirrored
The ripening fruit.

Bliss in Sadness

Don't dry up, don't dry up,
Tears of heavenly love!
Oh, even to the eye that's half-dry,
How barren, how dead the world seems to be!
Don't dry up, don't dry up,
Tears of eternal love!

*

Dearest Lili,
For oh so long
You were all my joy
And all my song,
But now you're all my pain- and yet,
Even now you're all my song.

To Lili

In beloved valleys, on mountains capped with snow,
Your form was always near;
I saw it weave around me in light clouds,
I felt it in my heart.
I'm sensing here, how with almighty force
One heart can pull its mate,
And that in vain love seeks
From love to flee.

The Elf King

Who's riding so late through night and wind?
It is the father holding his child;
He has the boy secure in his arm,
He clasps him tightly, he keeps him warm. –

My son, why hide your face in such fear? –
Do you not, father, see the Elf King?
The Elf King with his crown and tail? –
My son, it's just a streak of mist. –

"Hey, my dear child, come, go with me!
Such lovely games shall I play with you then;
You'll find many colorful flowers on the shore,
My mother has many a garment of gold."

My father, my father, and do you not hear,
What Elf King is quietly promising me? –
Be calm, please stay calm, oh my child!
It's just withered leaves that stir in the wind. –

"Don't you want to join me, fine boy?
My daughters shall wait on you, hand and foot;
My daughters perform the round dance at night,
And will rock and dance and sing you to sleep."

My father, my father, do you not see
How Elf King's daughters haunt the dark glen? –
My son, my son, I see it so well;
The willows are glowing so pale and gray. –

"I love you- your sweet form entices me so;
And if you aren't willing, I'll have to use force."
My father, my father, he's seizing me now!
Elf King has hurt me, hurt me so bad! –

The father shudders, he rides with great haste,
And holds in his arms the sick, moaning child,
With exhausting effort, he reaches his farm;
But in his arms the child was dead.

The Fisherman

The water rushed, the water swelled,
A fisherman sat on its bank,
Tranquilly watched his fishing rod,
Cool to the very heart.
And as he sits and hearkens,
The waters rise and open,
And from their agitation,
There emerges, moist, a maiden.

She sang to him, she spoke to him:
"Why do you tempt my brood,
With human wit and human tricks,
Up to the warmth of death?
Oh, if you knew how cozy it is
For fish here in the depths,
You'd come right down, just as you are,
And only then be well.

Does the dear sun not refresh itself,
The moon, too, in the sea?
Does their face, returned by breathing waves,
Appear not twice as fair?
Doesn't the depth of sky entice,
The moist-transfigured blue?
Doesn't your own face tempt you down
To the eternal dew?"

The water rushed, the water swelled,
　　Wetting his naked foot;
His heart grew full of longing,
　As at a sweetheart's greeting.
She spoke to him, she sang to him,
　And now his day was done:
Half she pulled, and half he sank-
　And was never seen again.

To Charlotte von Stein

Why give us these eyes that probe so deeply
To behold our future with foreboding,
That we never fully trust our love,
Our earthly joy, in blissful self-delusion?
Why, oh fate, give us the power to see,
By feeling all the other's heart conceals,
And in the soul's strange maze of burrows
Find our true relationship?

Thousands, in their mindless haste,
Never truly know their own heart,
Wander aimlessly about, and then run
Hopelessly to pain that's unforeseen;
Rejoice again when full of fleeting joys
A dawn breaks with its rosy light.
To us alone, two poor and loving souls,
Is that mutual happiness denied:
To love each other without comprehension,
In the other see all that he never was,
Always freshly seeking joy of dreams
And trembling, too, within imagined peril.

Happy those absorbed by empty dreams!
Happy those with vain presentiments!
Every presence, every glance, alas,
Gives added strength to all our dreams and visions.
Tell me, what could fate have left for us?
How did it join us with such pure precision?
Ah, you were within some former life
My sister, or perhaps my loving wife-

Knowing every feature of my being,
Listening for my finest nerve's vibration,
You read me with a single glance,
Such as no other mortal eye could ever do.
Drop by drop, you cooled the fever of my blood
And gave direction to its aimless raging,
And within your angel arms my shattered heart
Found peace and was restored;
You held me fast with magic, light and airy,
Dallying away so many days.

What blessedness could ever equal those sweet hours,
When I lay grateful at your feet,
Felt my heart swell up against your heart,
Felt that I was noble in your eyes,
As my every sense was filled with light
And the torrent of my blood was calmed.

And of all this but a memory lives on
Around the unsure heart; it feels the old truth
Glowing still unchanged within it,
While its new state is a source of pain.
We seem to have no more than half a soul,
Brightest day for us has turned to dusk.
Fortunate that fate, though it may plague us,
Cannot alter what we are!

The only man you can love, Lida,
You want all for yourself, and rightly so.
He is also solely yours.
For since I am away from you,
The noisy motion of this too rapid life
Seems but a light gauze
Through which I still see your form
As if in clouds.
It glows for me, friendly and true,
As through the Aurora's flickering beams
Eternal stars shimmer.

Restless Love

Through snow and rain
And wind I'm plodding,
Through steaming chasms,
Through mist and vapor,
Moving on! Moving on!
Never finding rest.

I'd rather be struggling
Through suffering and pain
Than bear so much happiness
Filling my life.
This drawing and pulling
Of hearts to each other,
How strangely it causes
Its own brand of pain.

What? Should I flee?
Escape to the woods?
All is in vain!
Crown of all life,
Joy without peace,
Love- that is you.

Hunter's Evening Song

Crazed and mute, I slip through fields,
My musket set to fire,
And there your sweet, beloved face
Floats down to me- as light.

In gentle stillness, you now walk
Through cherished field and glen;
And does my quickly fading face
Not once appear to you?

The face of one who combs the earth,
Sick with spleen and gall,
Wandering to the east and west
Because he can't have you.

I think of you and feel that I am
Gazing at the moon;
A quiet peace comes over me,
I don't know who I am.

Forever

Whatever man within his earthly limits
Of highest fortune calls by godly names,
The harmony of faith that can't be shaken,
Of friendship never plagued by care or doubt,
The light, that burns but for the wise in private thoughts,
For poets in their images of beauty,
All this I had discovered in my finest
Hours in her, and found what I'd been seeking.

To the Moon

Again you fill both bush and vale
With quiet misty light,
Finally too you cause my soul
To melt and be released.

Upon my field you spread out wide
Your gentle, healing glance,
Like my dear one's eyes that softly
Rest upon my fate.

Every echo strikes my heart
Of bright and gloomy times,
I wander between joy and pain,
In my solitude.

Flow, flow on, beloved stream!
I won't feel joy again,
So did play and kisses rush
Away- along with faith.

Yet I once possessed it all,
What one holds so dear,
Alas that to our torment
We cannot forget its worth!

Rush along the valley, stream,
Restless endlessly,
Rush and whisper for my song
A fitting melody.

When upon a winter's night,
You rage and flood your banks,
Or in spring's rich splendor
Well and curl around young buds.

Blessed he, who without hatred,
Shuts the world away,
Holds a friend close to his heart
And with this soul enjoys

That which other men have never
Known or never thought,
What through the heart's great labyrinth
Wanders in the night.

Harz Journey in Winter

Like a hawk,
Which rests on heavy morning
Clouds with gentle wings,
Searching for prey,
Let my song glide.

For a god has
Prescribed to
Each of us a path,
Which the fortunate
Run quickly
To goals that bring them joy;
But he whose heart
Adversity has squeezed,
He fights in vain
Against the fetters
Of that brazen thread,
Which only bitter shears
Will one day cut.

In shuddering thickets
The wild boar has fled,
And with the sparrows
The wealthy, too, have
Sunk into their swamps.

How easy to follow the carriage
Which good fortune leads,
Like the comfortable entourage
Of a prince, on roads
That are cleared before him.

But to the side there, who is it?
In undergrowth his path disappears,
Behind him the shrubbery
Closes together,
The grass stands up again,
The wasteland engulfs him.

Oh, who will heal the pain of one
Whose balm turns to poison,
Who has drunk human loathing
From the fullness of love?
First despised, now a despiser,
He secretly gnaws
Away at his worth
In self-seeking ways that lead nowhere.

If, in your Psalter,
Father of love, there's a tone
That can still reach his ear,
Bring succor and strength to his heart!
Open up his clouded eyes
To the thousand fountains
Surrounding the thirsting man
In the desert.

You who create countless joys,
For each of us more than enough,
Bless those joined in the hunt,
On the trail of the boar,
With that youthful, wanton
Delight in the kill,
Belated avengers of mischief,
Which the peasant for years
Has vainly fought off with a cane.

But wrap the lonely one
In your golden cloud,
Surround with wintergreen,
Till the rose again blooms,
The exposed wet hair,
Oh love, of your poet!

With your torch's faint glow
You light his way
Through the fords at night,
Over groundless paths
On barren fields,
With the thousand-colored morning
You laugh into his heart;
With your biting storms
You lift him up high.
Winter streams fall from rocks
Into his psalms,
And into an altar of sweetest thanks
That dreaded bald summit,
Hanging with snow, is transformed,
Which folk superstition
Used to inhabit with spirits and demons.

You stand there with heart unexplored,
Open in your mystery,
Above the astonished world,
And gaze from clouds
At its realms and glory,
Which you feed from the veins
Of your brothers beside you.

Take to Heart

Tell me, what should man desire?
Is staying at rest the better way?
Clambering to hold on tightly?
Or should he drive himself instead?
Should he build himself a cabin?
Should he dwell beneath a tent?
Should he put his trust in rock?
The most solid rock can quake.

No one thing is fit for all.
Let each one see what suits him best,
Let each one see where he should linger,
And who stands, that he not tumble.

Reminder

Why must you continue wandering?
See, the good- it lies so near.
Simply learn to grasp at joy,
For that joy is always there.

Cowardly thinking,
Scared vacillation,
Weak hesitation,
Anxious lamenting,
Ward off no misery,
Won't make you free.

Facing all powers
With steadfast defiance,
Not bowing down,
Showing your strength,
That is what brings
The embrace of the gods.

Drops of Nectar

When Minerva, to show favor
To her protégé, Prometheus,
Brought down from the lofty sky
A bowl that brimmed with sparkling nectar,
So that he might bring his humans
Joy, and kindle in their hearts
A passion for those sacred arts,
Swift of foot she hurried down,
Lest she be seen by Jupiter,
And the golden bowl then tilted
And a few drops of that nectar
Fell upon the soft green earth.

Busily the bees were on it,
Sucked it up with joyous effort,
Equally industrious,
The butterfly then stole its drop,
Even the misshapen spider
Crept to it and sucked with force.

Fortunate these drinkers were,
They and other tender creatures,
For they now share with us humans
The highest fortune- that of art.

Wanderer's Night Song (#1)

You who come from heaven
Can alleviate all pain and sorrow,
For the doubly wretched
You revive the heart with twice the spring.
Oh how sick I am of turmoil,
What end is served by pain and joy?
Sweetest peace,
Come, oh come into my breast!

Wanderer's Night Song (#2)

Over all the hilltops
There's peace,
In all the treetops
You detect
Hardly a breath;
The birds in the forest are silent.
Only wait, soon you'll
Also find rest.

Song of the Spirits over the Waters

The human soul
Is like the water:
It comes from heaven,
Ascends to heaven,
And down again
To earth it must fall,
Always shifting.

If from the steep and
Lofty rock face
The pure jet pours,
It breaks as spray into
Lovely cloud-waves
To touch smooth stone,
And gently welcomed
It undulates veiling,
Murmuring
To the depths below.

If jagged outcroppings
Fight its fall,
It foams in anger
Stepwise
To the abyss.

On level meadow beds
It creeps through the valley,
And in the smooth, clear lake
Every star in the sky
Lets its image go grazing.

Wind is the wave's
Delightful companion;
Wind stirs completely
Each foaming surge.

Oh human soul,
How like the water!
Oh human fate,
How like the wind!

Human Limits

When the holy
Primeval father,
With tranquil hand
From billowing clouds
Sows benediction
Of lightning upon the earth,
I kiss the trailing
Hem of his garment,
With the trembling faith of a
Child in my breast.

For with gods
No man should ever
Dare to compete.
If he lifts himself up
To touch
The stars with his crown,
His unsteady feet find
No surface to hold them,
As clouds and wind
Make him their plaything.

Standing with solid,
Marrowy bones
On the well-established
Permanent earth,
He doesn't succeed
In matching the oak or
Even the slender
Vine with his stature.

What distinguishes
Gods from men?
That many waves
Roll forth from the gods,
A timeless stream:
The wave, it lifts us,
The wave engulfs us
And so we sink.

A tiny ring
Limits our life,
And thus generations
Are constantly linked
To the endless chain
Of the gods' existence.

My Goddess

To which immortal
Should one give the highest praise?
I quarrel with no one,
But I award it to
The always new
And agile one,
The strangest of Jove's daughters,
His darling child
Imagination.

To her he's granted
All the moods
He'd otherwise
Keep for himself,
And in this foolish girl
He takes
His greatest joy.

Enwreathed in roses,
Lily-stem in hand,
She may walk through flower valleys,
Command the summer birds,
And suck the dew's light sustenance
With bee's lips
Out of blossoms.

Or at times she'll howl
With flying hair
And gloomy eyes
Through wind around
The walls of cliffs
And in myriad colors,
Like morning and evening,
Ever changing
Like the moon,
Shine her light on us mortals.

Let us all then
Praise the father,
The ancient, lofty one,
Who chose to give
This fair, unfading wife
To men, whose fate
Is to die.
To us alone
He's bound her
By eternal laws,
Commanding her,
In joy and squalor,
As a faithful spouse
To stay at our side.

All the other
Wretched creatures
Of the living earth,
So rich in children,
Wander and range
In the darker pleasure
And dismal pain
Of life bound
To the moment,
Bent by the yoke
Of mere physical need.

But we've been granted
His most supple
And coddled daughter-
What cause to rejoice!
Approach her with warmth
As you would a beloved,
Give her a woman's
Honor at home.

And don't let old wisdom,
That mother-in-law,
Ever offend
This delicate soul!

Yet I do know her sister,
More mature and composed,
My quiet and peaceful friend:
May she only turn
Away from me
With the light of my life,
The noble one who drives
And consoles- hope.

"Clara's Song" (from *Egmont*)

Sorrowful,
Joyful,
And so full of thoughts,
Anxiously
Reaching
In unresolved pain,
Rejoicing to heaven
And grieved unto death,
Happy alone
Is the soul that's in love.

From "Roman Elegies"

I

Say something to me, oh stones! Lofty palaces, will you not speak?
Streets, just utter a word! Spirit, are you not stirring?
Yes, there's a soul at work in all of your sacred walls,
Eternal Rome; for me alone it still remains silent.
Oh, who will whisper to me, at which window will I
Behold that sweet girl, who will refresh me with fire?
Don't I yet sense the paths by which, again and again,
Walking to her and from her, I'll offer up precious time?
Still I examine palace and church, pillars and ruins,
Just as a cautious man makes good use of his travels.
But soon all that will pass; and then a single temple,
The temple of love will stand, to receive its initiate.
You are a world indeed, oh Rome, but without love
The world would not be the world, and Rome would never be Rome.

II

When you tell me, girl, that when you were a child, folks did not find you
Appealing, and that even your mother would scorn you,
Until you'd grown up and developed in stillness-this I believe:
I think of you all too gladly as an exceptional child.
For even though the vine's blossom be lacking in form and color,
It's sure to delight both gods and men, when its berry turns ripe.

III

Feel no regret, my love, that you gave yourself to me so quickly!
   Believe me- no base or insolent thought crosses my mind.
  The arrows of Amor work in various ways: Some of them
Tear, and from creeping poison the heart becomes sick for years.
But with powerful feathers, and a freshly polished sharpness,
  Others bore into the marrow, igniting the blood with a bang.
   In the age of heroes, when gods and goddesses loved,
  Desire would follow a glance, enjoyment would follow desire.
  Do you think the goddess of love sat there and pondered,
    When in Ida's grove Anchises delighted her eye?
    If Luna had waited to kiss that beautiful sleeper,
  Then quickly Aurora, in envy, would have awakened the boy.
   Hero caught sight of Leander at that riotous feast,
And at once the lover's heat plunged him into the nocturnal flood.
   Rhea Silvia, the virginal princess, walks to the Tiber
  To fetch a bucket of water, and she is seized by the god.
Thus did Mars beget his two sons!- The twins drink the milk
  Of a wolf, and Rome declares itself queen of the world.

IV

See how the pastoral fire casts up its autumnal glow!
  Crackles and flickers so fast! Roars up from kindling so high!
  Tonight it brings me twice as much joy; for hours before
The bundle's consumed down to charcoal, sinks under ash,
My darling girl will have come. Then branches and twigs will flare,
  And the warmed up night will become a feast full of light.
When morning breaks, she'll quickly slip out of the lair of love,
  Energetically wake from the ashes flames that will rage anew.
  For Amor has given that flattering girl more than others:
  Power to bring back to life joy that has just sunk to ash.

V

Happy I feel, and inspired, here on this classical soil;
Past and present are speaking to me with more audible magic.
Here I follow the counsel, leaf through the works of the ancients
With a vigorous hand, each day with greater enjoyment.
But through the nights, I'm kept differently busy by love;
And am I not learning, by tracing the lovely shape of her breasts,
And sliding my hand down the curve of her hips?
Only then do I truly know marble; I think and compare,
See with an eye that can feel, feel with a hand that can see.
So what if my darling robs me of a few measly hours of the day?
She gives me hours of the night, which compensate more than enough.
And then, we are not always kissing, we talk about serious things;
And when sleep overcomes her, I lie there and think a great deal.
Often, too, I've actually composed some verse in her arms,
And tapped the hexameter's beat, softly with fingering hand,
Out on her naked back. She lies there in beautiful slumber,
And the warmth of her breath burns to the depths of my heart.
Meanwhile Amor rekindles the lamp, and thinks of the days
When he'd perform that same task for his triumvirate of poets.

From "Venetian Epigrams"

Yes, there is much I can stand. Most things hard or annoying
I endure in brave silence, just as a god commands.
A few, however, are loathsome to me as poison or snakes-
Four of them: smoke from tobacco, bedbugs, garlic and Christians.

*

"Billy goats, off to the left!" The judge will one day decree;
"And you, little lambs, feel free to stand to my right!"
Very well! But one more thing can be hoped; he'll then
Say: "You men of sense, I want you to stand here and face me."

*

The dreamer finds himself plenty of pupils and moves the big crowd,
While the man of sense surrounds himself with the few.
Miracle working pictures are mostly inferior paintings:
Works of the mind and of art are simply not there for the mob.

*

Let all gushing dreamers be nailed to the cross by their thirtieth year!
Once they have seen through the world, the disillusioned turn scoundrel.

*

"Don't be so insolent, epigrams!" And tell us why not? We are
Only the epigraphs; the chapters belong to the world.

*

Insolent I have become; and it's no wonder. You gods
Know, and you're not alone, I'm pious and faithful as well.

*

All those apostles of freedom were always anathema to me,
To exercise his own whim is all each one sought in the end.
If you wish to free many, then dare to give service to many.
How much risk is involved? If you are curious, try!

*

France's tragic fate- let the great of the world give it thought!
But truly the small should ponder it even more.
Great ones went to their death; but who will protect
The mob from the mob? The mob then became the mob's tyrant.

*

Do not be angry, women, that we admire a girl:
What she has stirred in the evening, you will enjoy at night.

*

Boys I could also love, but I am much fonder of girls:
When I grow tired of her girlhood, she still can serve as a boy.

*

It doesn't surprise me that Christ our Lord liked to consort
With harlots and people who sinned; you see, it's the same way with me.

*

"If I were a housewife, and had all the things that I needed,
I'd be happy and faithful, hugging and kissing my man."
Thus sang, among other vulgar songs, a whore
To me in Venice; and I've never heard a prayer more pious.

*

You inspired me with love and desire; I feel it and burn.
Lovable girl, now inspire me with trust.

*

Do not fear, oh lovely girl, the snake that draws near you!
Eve, she knew it already; just ask the preacher, my child.

*

Do not turn, lovely girl, your slender legs to the sky.
Zeus, that rascal, might see you- and Ganymede is concerned.

*

Go ahead, and turn your feet to the sky without worry!
We lift our arms in prayer, but never so innocently.

*

Whether or not the words that were spoken by Moses and prophets
Find their fulfillment in Christ- friend, I really don't know;
But I know this: Fulfilled are wishes, longing and dreams,
Whenever that lovely girl sweetly sleeps at my side.

*

The girl was poor and unclothed when she first entered my life;
Back then her nakedness pleased me, as it delights me today.

*

Tell me, how are you living? I'm living! And if man
Could live for hundreds of years, I'd wish each day like today.

Euphrosyne

Even from the highest mountains' jagged ice-covered peaks
The purple glow of the setting sun rapidly fades away.
Night has already covered the valley and paths of the wanderer,
Who, by the raging stream, longs to ascend to his hut,
To the goal of the day, the quiet pastoral dwelling,
And god-like sleep, always pleasing, hurries to get there before him,
That dear companion of travelers; if only today he would
Bless my head with the wreath of his sacred poppy!
But what radiance is it that glows for me there from the rocks,
Brightening the mist of the foaming streams with such warmth?
Is the sun perhaps shining through mysterious fissures and gaps?
For it's no earthly glow, that wandering one over there.
The cloud's moving nearer, pulsing with warmth, I gape at its wonder!
Is the rose-colored beam not becoming a shape full of life?
What goddess could be approaching me, and which of the muses
Seeks her true friend, here in vertiginous gorges?
Fairest goddess! Reveal yourself to me, and don't disappoint,
Disappearing, the mind that's inspired, the heart that's been moved!
Give me, if you may grant this to mortals, your godly name,
Or, if not, then stir me and shake me with meaning,
That I might feel which of the heavenly daughters of Zeus
You might be, and the poet might worthily praise you in song.
"Have you forgotten me, dear one, and could this form, that you
Once held so dear, be just a strange image already?
Of course, I no longer belong to the earth, and the shuddering spirit's
Been mournfully ripped from the cheerful enjoyment of youth,
But I'd still hoped to find my picture engraved in the memory
Of friends, and transfigured in beauty by love.
Yes, already your eyes' emotion, your tears- they are saying:
Euphrosyne, she's still recognized by her friend.

See, the departing one passes through forest and frightening mountains,
Seeks the wandering man, alas, in the distance once more,
Seeks the teacher, the friend, the father, looks back once again
On the flimsy frame of the fleeting joys of the earth.
Let me think of the days when I, still a child, entered the mysteries
Of theater- of the magical muses' art of illusion- with you.
Let me think of the hours, each detail, however small it might seem.
Oh, who wouldn't call back that which can never return!
That sweet, friendly throng of the lightest of earthly days, who fully
Appreciates, as it deserves, this good that rushes on past us!
Small it appears to us now, but to the heart never petty;
Don't love and art make everything small appear great?
Remember that time, on the scaffolding's boards, how you helped me
To take my first steps in that lofty dramatic art?
I appeared as a boy, a pitiful child; Arthur you called me- and
Animated within me the poetic world of a Briton,
Threatening my poor eyes with a violent brand, you turned
Away your own tearful glance, shaken by the deception.
Oh, how dear you were then, protecting a life full of sadness,
Which a reckless flight finally tore from that boy.
In friendly arms you held me, the shattered one, carried me off,
And long did I lie at your bosom pretending to be really dead.
Finally I opened my eyes, and saw how you'd sunk into
Quiet, serious thought, as you stood there bent over your pupil.
Like a child I pulled myself up, gratefully kissing your hands,
Offering for the purest kiss my mouth, that was ready to please,
Asking: Why, my father, so grave? And if I've done wrong,
Then show me how I might better succeed in the future!
No effort ever annoys me with you, and joyfully will I
Repeat every task, as long as you guide and teach me.
But your strong arms kept holding me, pressing me closer,
And deep in my breast I felt my own heart as it shuddered.
No, my delightful child! you exclaimed, every little
Thing you've shown here, show the whole city tomorrow.

Move them all, as you have moved me, and for your applause
Glorious tears will flow from the driest of eyes.
But you deeply affected the friend holding you here in his arms,
Who was terrified by the mere appearance of premature death.
Nature, alas, how great and sure you appear in all things!
Heaven and earth, they both obey laws that are solid, eternal,
Years follow the years, spring gives the summer its hand,
As fall, the abundant one, graciously does for the winter.
Rocks on foundations stand, and waters eternal fall
Foaming and roaring, down from the cloudy crevasse.
Spruces are ever green, and even the leafless bushes bear,
In winter already, those secret buds on their branches.
All things emerge and pass according to law, but on human
Life, that valuable treasure, a tottering fate seems to reign.
Not always does it occur that the father, ready to pass,
Gives a kind nod from the edge to his noble son full of life;
It isn't always the young and strong who close the eyes
Of the old and frail, who are ready to close them themselves.
Fate too often, alas, perverts the order of days;
Helplessly and in vain, an old man wails for his children,
Or grandchildren, a damaged trunk, surrounded by splintered
Branches, strewn about by torrents of deadly hail.
And so, delightful child, I fell into contemplation
When you, disguised as a corpse, lay hanging over my arms;
But with gladness I see you, dearest one, full of life once again,
In the radiance of youth, here so close to my heart.
So, cheerfully skip away, would-be boy, as the girl grows up
To the joy of the world and, yes, to my greater delight.
Continue to strive as you do, and mold nature's gifts,
Through each step of life, to the highest standards of art.
May you long give me pleasure, and before my eye closes, I hope
To see your beautiful talent happily reach its perfection.—
So you spoke, and I never forgot that important hour,
Pondering your sublime advice, I continued to grow.

With what gladness I brought to the people those speeches so moving
　　And deep, entrusted by you to the lips of a child.
　　I molded myself, watching your eyes, seeking you out
　　In that dense mob of people, who listened astonished.
　　But now, when you stand there, no longer will Euphrosyne
　　Come forward, to bring a bright cheer to your eyes.
You'll hear them no more, those tones from a growing disciple,
Whom you taught to feel all too early- that pain that is born out of love.
　　Others will come and go, others are going to please you,
　　Even great talent gets pushed to the side by one greater.
　　But you, oh don't you forget me! If ever a girl
　　Moves cheerfully toward you in the hub-hub of daily affairs,
　　Follows your signal, takes joy in your smile, and is happy only
　　　When she's in that place that you have assigned her,
　　Who spares nothing, no effort at all, her powers all active,
　　Even bringing her offering of joy to the edge of the grave-
　　Good man, do think of me then, crying out, though it's too late:
　　　Euphrosyne, she's risen again here before me!
There is much I would still like to say, but the parting one can't linger on
　　As she'd wish; already a lingering haste draws me onward.
　　Just hear my one wish, and grant it as a good friend:
Don't let me descend to the shadows thinking the world will forget me!
　　Only the muses can give us a kind of life after death.
　　For formlessly in Persephone's realm, masses of shades
　　　Hover around, divorced from their names;
But she who is praised by a poet, the one who forms and transforms,
That woman will join the chorus of heroes, remaining a singular being.
　　Joyfully will I step forward, announced to them all by your song,
　　And the goddess' eye will linger upon me with pleasure.
　　Gently she will welcome me then, and name me, while other
　　Deified women, those nearest the throne, will point to me too.
　　Penelope then will address me, that most faithful of women,
　　Euadne, too, as she leans on that spouse she loves so much.
Younger ones then will approach, those who were sent down too early,

And with me they will lament the fate we were forced to share.
When Antigone comes, of souls the most sisterly one,
And Polyxena, still grieved by her virginal death,
I'll look at them all as sisters, walking in dignity toward them.
If only a poet could capture me too, his songs,
They would perfect in me, that which my life has denied me."
Thus she spoke, and her lovely mouth kept on moving a while,
As if still to speak; but the tones buzzed away into nothing.
For out of the purple cloud that still hovered, constantly shifting,
Hermes, the glorious god, calmly emerged and stepped forward.
Gently he lifted his staff and pointed; the cloud swelled in waves
And engulfed, in a flash, both of the figures before me.
Deeper night envelops me now, the plummeting waters
Are rushing more fiercely along my slippery path.
An irresistible, strength-draining anguish seizes my being,
And only a mossy stone gives me support as I collapse.
A sadness tears at the strings of my heart, tears flow all night,
Until over the woods morning begins to announce its approach.

Art and nature seem to flee each other
And come to reunite before you know it.
For me, as well, there is no more aversion,
And both appear to draw me equally.

The only goal is honest, open effort,
And only when we've bound ourselves to art,
In measured hours, with diligence and spirit,
Can nature freely glow within our hearts.

So it is with every form of culture.
It is in vain that all unfettered spirits
Strive for the perfection of pure summits.

Those who'd seek what's great must find their center.
The master first reveals himself in limits,
And only law can ever give us freedom.

Coptic Song

Go! And let me be your beacon:
Learn to use those days of youth,
   And be wiser while you can.
   On the giant scale of fortune
   Rarely does the pointer rest.
   You must rise or you must fall;
You must hold the power and win
Or you'll lose and play the servant,
   You must suffer loss or triumph,
      Be an anvil or a hammer.

Hard to Get

On the purest of spring mornings
Walked the shepherdess and sang,
Young and fair and without worry,
That it rang throughout the fields:

"So la la, so la la..."

Thyrsis offered for some kisses
Two, no three lambs on the spot.
Roguishly she looked a moment,
But she sang and laughed away:

"So la la, so la la..."

And another offered ribbons,
And a third one bid his heart,
But she made fun of heart and ribbons,
As she'd ridiculed the lambs:

"So la la, so la la..."

Converted

By the crimson glow of evening
I walked quietly by the wood.
Damon sat and played his flute,
That it echoed from the rocks:

"So la la, so la la..."

And he pulled me down to him,
Kissed me tenderly and sweetly,
And I said: "Oh, play again!"
And the good boy piped away:

"So la la, so la la..."

Now my peace of mind forsakes me
And my joy is also gone,
And all I hear before my ears
Is that constant, ancient tone:

"So la la, so la la..."

Her Beloved is Near

I think about you, when the sun's bright shimmer
From ocean streams.
I think about you, when the moon's soft flicker
Is caught in springs.

I see you, when upon those distant pathways
The dust clouds rise,
In darkest night, when on the narrow footbridge
The wanderer quakes.

I hear you, when with muted roar and sizzle
The wave swells up.
In quiet groves I often walk to listen,
When all is still.

I am with you, and though you be so distant,
To me you're near!
The sun goes down, the stars will soon be glowing-
I want you here!

May Song

Between wheat field and corn,
Between hedges and thorn,
Between meadow and trees,
Where's she walking?
Tell me this!

I did not find my
Dear one home,
That golden girl
Must be outside.
Green and fair
The May is blooming;
Darling wanders
Glad and free.

On the rocks by the stream,
Where she offered that kiss,
Yes, the first in the grass,
I see something!
Is it she?

Presence

All things announce your approach!
When the glorious sun shows its face,
You'll follow, so I hope, soon.

When you step forth in the garden,
Then you're the rose of all roses,
Lily of lilies as well.

Whenever you move in a dance,
Then all of the stars move
With and around you in circles.

Night! And so let it be night!
Now you outshine the lovely,
Bestowing light of the moon.

Bestowing and lovely you are,
And flowers, moon and stars
Pay homage, sun, only to you.

Sun! May you be for me too
A creator of glorious days,
Where life and eternity merge.

Discovered

I strolled through the woods,
Just on a whim,
Not seeking anything,
That was my plan.

In the shade I saw
A flower so small,
That glowed like a star,
As lovely as eyes.

When I tried to pick it,
It charmingly said:
"Is it merely to wither
That I'm being picked?"

I then dug it out
With all of its roots,
Found a garden patch,
By a quaint little house.

I replanted it there
In that quiet spot,
Now it keeps sprouting twigs
And continues to bloom.

The God and the Bayadera

Mahadeyu, lord of earth,
Comes down again for the sixth time,
That he might become like us,
To feel our happiness and pain.
He condescends to dwell down here,
Lets all things happen as they will,
For if he's meant to spare or punish,
He must view humans as a man.
And when, as a wanderer, he's looked at a city,
Spied on the great and regarded the small,
He leaves it at evening to go on his way.

And now, when he has walked far out
To where the lowest houses are,
He sees with brightly painted cheeks
A child, lost and beautiful.
"Greetings, maiden!" "Thank-you, sir!
Wait, and I will be right out!"
"And who are you?" "Bayadera,
And this is the house of love."
She stirs as she beats her cymbals for dancing,
She knows how to move in the loveliest circles,
She nods and she bows as she hands him some flowers.

Coaxing him up to the door,
She pulls her guest into the house.
"Fairest stranger, bright with lamps
This hut will be, before you know it.
If you're tired, I'll refresh you,
Soothe the pain within your feet.
What you want, you shall have,
Be it rest or games or pleasure."
She busily tends to the suffering he feigns.
The godly one smiles; he sees with great joy,
Through depravity's depths, a heart that is human.

He demands full servitude,
But her cheerfulness increases,
And what had been her art before
Gradually becomes her nature.
And so upon the blossom
There appears, in proper time, the fruit:
If obedience is in the heart,
Love cannot be far away.
But to test her more sharply and thoroughly now,
He who knows both what is highest and lowest
Decides to let her taste joy and despair.

And he kisses her bright cheeks,
And she feels the throb of love,
And the girl becomes a captive,
And she cries for the first time.
She falls down at his feet,
Not for ecstasy or profit,
And, alas, her supple limbs
Refuse to do her bidding.
And so, for the pleasurable feast of the bed,
The night now prepares the beautiful web
Of that veil which gives welcome comfort to all.

Late to sleep amid caresses,
Waking early from short rest,
At her side she finds him dead,
That guest she's grown to love so much.
And she falls upon him, screaming,
But she cannot wake him up,
And they carry his stiff limbs
To that dreaded pit of fire.
She hears the priests and their funeral chants.
Raving, she runs through the crowd, which gives way:
"Who are you? And what brings you here to the grave?"

Falling down beside the litter,
She fills the air with piercing cries.
"I want my husband back,
And I seek him in his tomb!
Should the splendor of his limbs
Turn to ash before my eyes?
He was mine! And no one else's!
Why, oh why, just one sweet night!"
The priests are chanting, "We carry the old,
Who long have been weak and now have grown cold,
We carry the young, who expect it the least.

Listen to your priests' stern teaching:
This man here was not your husband.
Living as a bayadera
Frees you from all obligation.
The shade alone pursues the body
Down into the realm of death,
Only wives can follow husbands,
That is both their fame and duty.
Sound out, oh trumpets, for sacred lamenting,
And take, you gods, this jewel of the day,
Take this youth to yourselves in flames!"

So the chorus, without mercy,
Adds to all her heart's distress,
And stretching out her arms, she leaps
Into the furnace of her death.
But the godly youth emerges,
Rising up above the flame,
And his dear one, too, appears,
Floating upward in his arms.
The godhead rejoices in sinners' repentance,
And the immortal ones lift their lost children,
With fiery arms, to their heaven above.

Immense Astonishment

From cloud-enshrouded caverns' halls- a stream,
Impatient for its union with the ocean,
Comes rushing forth; ignoring all that's mirrored
On its depths, it heads straight toward the valley.

But all at once the oread, force demonic,
With woods and mountain following in whirlwinds-
She plunges in to take her cooling pleasure.
She checks its course, confines the widening basin.

The wave breaks into spray, surprised, withdrawing,
Swells up, the constant draught of its own drinking;
Its striving toward the father is impeded.

It rocks and rests, dammed up into a lake now;
The stars, reflected, contemplate the sparkle
Of waves that lap the rocks, a new life's dawning.

Hegira

North and West and South are splitting,
Thrones explode and realms are trembling,
Flee then you- to taste in clear, pure
East the air of patriarchs;
While you love and drink and sing,
You'll find youth in Chiser's fountain.

There, in cleanliness and rightness,
I shall probe into the depths
Of primeval human races,
When they still received from God
Heaven's word in earthly language,
Without cracking up their heads.

When they still revered their fathers
And resisted foreign service.
I'll rejoice in fettered youth,
Wide in faith, in thinking narrow,
Where the word still carried weight,
Because the word was "spoken".

I'll associate with herdsmen,
Find refreshment in oases,
When with caravans I wander,
Selling shawls and musk and coffee.
Every path I'll seek to follow
From the desert to the cities.

Up and down those wicked rock-ways
    Hafiz' songs will give me comfort,
        When the driver, with delight,
        From the high back of the mule,
        Sings to coax the stars awake
        And frighten off the robbers.

    When I stop at baths and taverns,
        I'll think of you, oh holy Hafiz,
        When my dear girl lifts her veil
    To shake sweet curls of ambergris.
        Let the poet's loving whispers
        Make the very houris lustful.

    Should you choose to envy him
Or even spoil his joy, you need to know:
        The words that poets speak
    Are always floating, softly knocking,
        Around the door of paradise,
        Begging for eternal life.

Unlimited

That you cannot end, that makes you great,
Nor ever begin, that is your fate.
Your song revolves like the vault of stars,
Beginning and ending always the same,
And what the middle brings is that
Which remains in the end and was when it began.

You are the true poetic font of joy,
That sends out wave upon countless wave;
A mouth that's always ready to kiss,
A song flowing sweetly from your breast,
A gullet always primed to drink,
A benevolent heart, that pours itself out.

And should the whole world sink to nothingness,
With you, oh Hafiz, with you alone
Will I compete! Joy and pain,
Let them be our common lot, as twins.
It shall be my pride, my life,
To love and drink like you.

Now ring out, song, with your own fire!
For you are older, you are newer.

Creation and Animation

Old Adam was a clod of earth
Which God made into human,
And he continued to pull many
Hulks from Mother's womb.

The Elohim, into his nose
They blew the best of spirits,
And now he seemed to be much more,
For he began to sneeze.

But with his bones and limbs and head,
He still was half a clump,
Until Noah, for that ninny,
Finally found the truth- the goblet.

The clump begins to feel the verve,
As soon as he wets his whistle,
Just as dough, through fermentation,
Sets itself in motion.

So, Hafiz, let your friendly song,
Your holiest example,
Lead us by the glasses' clang
To our creator's temple.

Past in the Present

Rose and lily, moist with morning,
Bloom within this garden near me.
Beyond this- sheltered by its bushes,
A cliff juts out against the sky.
Surrounded by a lofty forest,
With medieval castle crowned,
The summit's arc extends
Until it makes peace with the valley.

And there it smells of former days,
When we suffered still for love,
And my Psalter's strings competed
With the radiance of the morning,
Where the hunter's song from bushes
Breathed a tone of round abundance,
To inspire and to refresh,
As the heart desired and needed.

Now that they eternally flourish,
Take your courage from these forests.
What you once enjoyed yourselves,
In others, too, can be enjoyed.
No one then can cry against us
That we keep it for ourselves;
Now in every stage of life
You must be able to enjoy.

And with this song and turning point,
We find ourselves again with Hafiz,
For it's fitting to enjoy
The day's completion with enjoyers.

To Hafiz

What all desire, you know already,
And well you've understood:
That longing holds us all, from dust
To throne, in iron chains.

It hurts so much, then feels so good,
Who'd ever dare resist it?
And even if one broke his neck,
The other one stayed reckless.

Forgive me, master, for you know
How often I transgress,
When she, the wandering cypress,
Tears my eye in her direction.

Like fibrous roots her foot creeps forth,
Flirting with the ground,
As light as clouds her greeting melts,
Her breath like east wind's fondling.

All this surges at us strangely,
Where curl locks into curl,
Swelling in rings of auburn fullness,
To wisp then in the wind.

Now her forehead is unveiled,
To level out your heart.
You hear a song so true and glad,
In which to bed your spirit.

Then her lips begin to move
In a most adorable way,
And at once they set you free
To lay yourself in fetters.

Your breath no longer seeks its home,
As soul flees into soul,
As through your joy a fragrance winds,
Passing through cloud unseen.

But when it burns too brightly,
Your hands reach for the wine bowl.
The steward runs, the steward comes,
A first and second time.

His eye is flashing, heart is trembling,
He hopes to learn from you,
To hear you in the highest sense,
When wine has raised your spirits.

He sees the cosmic spaces open,
Within him health and order.
His chest then swells, his beard turns brown:
He has become a man.

And if no secret of the heart
Or world is kept from you,
You beckon kindly to the thinker
That his mind might flower completely.

And so that we might never miss
The kind support of princes,
You say a good word to the Shah,
And one to his officials.

You know all this, and sing of it
Today and, yes, tomorrow,
And thus your friendly company carries
Us through life's rough sweetness.

Universal Life

Dust, oh Hafiz, is among those
Elements your magic masters,
When in honor of your dear one
You intone a graceful song.

For the dust upon her threshold
Is more precious than that carpet
On the gold-wrought flowers of which
Mohammed's favored ones would kneel.

When wind blows lively clouds of dust
Toward you from your sweet girl's door,
To musk and rose oil you prefer
That rich and heady fragrance.

Dust...I've had to live without it
Up here in the cloudy north,
Whereas in the scorching south
I've had my ample share of it.

But too long now have my kind doors
Stayed so quiet on their hinges!
Heal me, storm rains! Let me breathe the
Scent of youthful, sprouting leaves!

Now with every roll of thunder,
While the sky is all aglow,
The wild dust of the wind is cast
As pollen's moisture to the ground.

And at once a life bursts forth,
A swelling action...secret, sacred;
Young leaves sprout and fill with green
The regions of the earth.

On luxuriant, bushy branches-
My love, just take a look!
Let yourself be shown the fruit
In shells of prickly green.

Balled up, they've long been hanging,
So still, apart, unknown.
A bough in swinging motion
Rocks them patiently.

But constantly the brown pit swells
And ripens from within.
He'd like to reach the air
And would gladly see the sun.

The shell then bursts and down
He falls, so glad to be set free.
Thus do my songs come dropping down
In piles, into your lap.

In a thousand forms you seek to hide yourself,
Yet most beloved one, at once I know it's you.
You might obscure yourself with veils of magic,
But omnipresent one, at once I know it's you.

In the purest youthful striving of the cypress,
Oh fairest growing one, at once I know it's you.
In the crystal living ripples of canals,
All-flattering one, it's clear to me it's you.

When the jet of water rises up unfolding,
All-playful one, I'm glad to see it's you.
When clouds take form and, shifting, change their form,
Oh many-sided one, there I know it's you.

On the flowered meadow-carpet of the veil,
All-motley starry one, as beauty I see you,
And in the circling grasp of rampant ivy,
Oh all-embracing one, there I know you.

When morning is ignited on the mountains,
At once, all-cheering one, I welcome you.
Then as the rounded sky spreads out above me,
All-heart-expanding one, then I breathe you.

What I know with senses outward, inward,
You all-informing one, I know through you,
And when I speak the hundred names of Allah,
Each one echoes back a name for you.

Locks of hair, keep me captive
  In the circle of her face!
To you brown, beloved serpents
  I have nothing to compare.

This heart alone is everlasting,
  Swells in fullest flower of youth.
Under snow and shrouds of mist,
  An Etna rises up to you.

Like the dawn, you put to shame
  That summit's all too earnest wall,
And once again old Hatem feels
The breath of spring and summer fire.

Tavern boy! Another bottle!
  This goblet here I'll bring to her.
  Should she find a pile of ash,
She will say, "He burned for me."

To Suleika

To caress you with sweet fragrance
And to elevate your joys,
A thousand budding roses first
Must perish in a blaze.

To possess a little flask
That might hold that scent forever,
Slender as your fingertips,
For that a world is needed...

A world of vital drives, which
In the pressure of their fullness,
Bulbul's loves already sensed,
Song to agitate the soul.

Should we rue such torment,
When it adds to our enjoyment?
Hasn't Timur's rule consumed
A thousand times as many souls?

Hatem

It's not chance that makes a thief,
She is herself the greatest thief,
For she stole the balance
Of the love remaining in my heart.

To you she has surrendered it,
All the profit of my life,
That I now, impoverished,
Owe this life to you alone.

But already I feel mercy
In the sparkle of your eyes,
And rejoice within your arms
In a destiny renewed.

Suleika

Made most happy by your love,
I cannot hold chance to blame;
For though she was a thief to you,
How much joy such robbing gives me!

And why, then, speak of robbery?
Give yourself to me by choice.
All too gladly would I think-
I was the one who stole your heart.

What you've given willingly
Brings you profit beyond measure;
The peace, the richness of my life,
I'm glad to give- take it! It's yours.

Don't joke. Speak not of poverty.
Does our love not make us rich?
If I hold you in my arms,
I'm as blessed as anyone.

Gingko Biloba

This tree's leaf, which from the east
Has been entrusted to my garden,
Lets one savor secret meaning
Such as edifies the knowing.

Is it just one living being
That has split itself in two?
Is it two that sought each other,
So that they'd be known as one?

To give answer to such questions
I have found the proper sense:
Don't you feel within my songs
That I am one and double too?

Lofty Image

The sun, Helios of the Greeks,
Rides in splendor through the sky,
So sure to win the universe,
He looks around, above, below.

He sees the fairest goddess weeping,
Cloud daughter, heaven's child;
For her alone he seems to shine—
Blind to every cheerful space,

He sinks into the pain of showers,
And her flow of tears increases;
He sends his joy into her pain,
And to each pearl- repeated kisses.

His glances' power she now feels deeply,
Steadily she lifts her gaze;
The pearls seek to assume a shape,
And each one takes his image.

Thus, enwreathed with arc and color,
Her face emits a cheerful glow,
As he in turn draws near her,
But alas! He cannot reach her.

And so, by some hard stroke of fate,
Beloved, you retreat from me,
And even if I were the sun,
What good would be my chariot throne?

Wanderer's Peace of Mind

Let no one complain about
What's vile and/or malicious;
It possesses all the power
Whatever folks might tell you.

In badness it holds sway
And profits from it greatly;
With rightness it can play,
Completely as it pleases.

Wanderer! You'd actually fight
This hopeless situation?
Whirlwind and dried excrement,
Let them spin and turn to dust!

Talisman

In breathing there are two kinds of grace:
Drawing air in, unloading its burden.
One can oppress, the other refresh;
Our life's this strange and wonderful mix.
So thank God, when you feel Him press,
And thank Him, when He releases His grip.

Phenomenon

When with the wall of rain
Phoebus has union,
At once an arc appears,
Colorfully shaded.

Through mist I sometimes see
A similar circle;
This arc may well be white,
But still a heaven's arc.

So, blithe old man, don't be
Needlessly troubled,
For though your hair be white,
Love will still find you.

(Spoken by Suleika)

What's the meaning of this motion?
Does the east wind bring glad tidings?
The fresh vibration of his wings
Cools the deep wounds of the heart.

Caressingly he plays with dust,
Casts it upward in light clouds,
Drives to vine leaves' sanctuary
The cheerful folk of little insects,

Gently tempers glowing sun rays,
Cools the fire of my own cheeks,
In his flight he kisses grapes
Which shine with life on hills and fields.

To me as well his whisper brings
So many greetings from my lover.
Before these hills are draped in darkness,
I'll be kissed a thousand times.

And so, you can continue moving,
Serve my friends and troubled souls.
There, where lofty walls are glowing,
I'll soon find my most beloved.

Oh, the true news of the heart,
The breath of love, of life's refreshment,
Can only come from his sweet mouth,
Can only issue from his breath.

Reunited

Can it be that, star of stars,
I once more press you to my heart!
Ah, what is the night of distance
    For a chasm of despair.
Yes, it's you! The sweet, beloved
    Counterpart to all my joys.
    Thinking of past suffering,
I shudder still before the present.

When the world in deepest regions
    Lay at God's eternal breast,
    He gave order to the first hour
    With sublime joy in creation.
And He uttered: "Let there be!"
    Then a cry of pain rang out,
    As the All, in violent motion,
        Broke into realities.

Light then opened up, and shyly
    Darkness shrank away from it,
        And at once the elements
        All separated, fell apart,
Rushing, struggling for the distance,
Through a bleak and savage dream,
    Frozen in unmeasured spaces,
Without longing, without sound.

All was mute, so still and desolate,
God alone for the first time.
Whereupon He made the Dawn-
She took pity on His pain.
She developed for the gloom
A play of colors, rich in music;
And now, what had just fallen apart,
Could find its way to love again.

And so, with hurried striving,
What belongs together seeks its kind,
And to life unmeasured
Both the eye and heart are turned.
Call it grasping, call it snatching,
Just as long as we hold on.
Allah need create no longer-
It is we who make His world.

Thus, with rose-wings of the dawn,
I was ripped back to your mouth,
And the night with countless seals
Gives star-bright strength to our alliance.
Both of us, upon the earth,
Are paragons of joy and pain,
And a second "Let there be!"
Will not split us up again.

Blessed Longing

Tell it only to the wise,
For the mob will surely scorn it.
I would praise that living being
Which longs for death in flames.

In the cooling of the love nights,
Which gave life, where you gave life,
An uncanny feeling fills you
When the quiet candle glows.

No longer are you kept embraced
Within the shades of darkness,
And a new desire consumes you
To a loftier coition.

Distance cannot weigh you down,
You're borne along and soar, transfixed,
And at last, of light desirous,
You are burned, oh butterfly.

And if this secret truth escapes you:
Die, and then become!
You are but a murky guest
Upon this gloomy earth.

Higher and Highest

That we dare to teach such things,
Will not, I hope, lead to our censure:
To have it all explained,
You simply ask your deepest self.

Then surely you will hear that man,
The object of his own love,
Longs to see his ego saved,
Both up above and here on earth.

My ego too would need
So many kinds of comfort,
Pleasures like I've sipped down here
I'd want to savor for all ages.

Thus will lovely gardens please us,
Flowers and fruit and comely maidens,
Just as in this world we loved them,
Shall we love them when renewed.

Likewise would I gladly gather
Young and old friends in one circle,
All stammering words of heaven
In my own beloved German.

But now we hear strange dialects
Of men and angels, softly necking,
Hidden grammar, new declensions,
Fragrant forms of rose and poppy.

And beyond this, one might speak
In glances' quiet rhetoric,
Rising up to heaven's trembling joys,
Devoid of sound or tone.

But tone and sound are soon released
Quite naturally from the word,
As sensing our infinitude
We are indeed transfigured.

If in such a way my separate
Senses can be gratified,
I'm sure to gain a single sense
That covers all of these.

And now I push in every space
More lightly through eternal circles,
Which are permeated
By the pure and living word of God.

Thus unencumbered, warmly driven,
There can be no end,
Until face to face with endless love
We float and fade away.

What kind of god would only push from outside,
   And let the world revolve around his finger?
It suits Him more to move the world from inside,
   Hold nature in Himself, Himself in nature,
So that everything that lives and weaves and is
   Might always feel His power and His spirit.

   Within us too there is a total world,
Which helps explain the worthy wont of peoples
   To give to everything they deem the best
The name God, indeed their God alone,
   Surrendering earth and sky to Him,
They fear Him- and love Him if they can.

Parabase

Years ago, and full of joy,
My mind would strive so zealously
To probe and to experience
How nature, by creating, lives.
And it's the eternal oneness
Manifested in the many,
Small the great, and great the small,
Each according to its kind.
Always shifting, holding fast,
Near and far and far and near;
Presenting form and changing form-
And I am here to gape in awe.

Epirrhema

You must, when contemplating nature,
Heed the one within the all;
Nothing's inside, nothing's outside:
For what's inside, that is outside.
So then grasp without delay
This sacred, open mystery.

Take joy in all this true appearance,
In the serious game;
Nothing living is a oneness,
Always it's a many.

From the "Proverbs"

I walk a wide and motley field
Of pure, primeval nature,
The lovely spring in which I bathe
Was handed down- as grace.

*

How? When? And Whither? –The gods are mute on this!
So stick to the Because, and cease to query: Why?

*

If you wish to cross the infinite,
Just walk the finite world in all directions.

*

If you seek refreshment from the whole,
You have to learn to see it in what's smallest.

*

Speak not of transience,
However it occurred!
To strive for eternity,
That's why we're here.

*

Why is it that God is so pleasing to us?
It's because he never gets in our way.

*

Understand
Without delay
What makes you struggle with this world;
It isn't heart it wants, but courtesy.

From "Wilhelm Tischbein's Idylls"

In the water-mirror's center
Rose the oak to lofty height,
A majestic, princely seal
To such verdant forest bloom;
Sees itself at its own feet,
Sees the sky within the flood:
To enjoy life in this manner
Solitude's the highest good.

From "German-Chinese Seasons"

I

So, what's left for mandarins,
Instead of ruling, tired of serving,
Say, what could be left for us,
Than on early days of spring
To thrust the north out of our minds
And by the water, on the green,
Drink with gladness, write with spirit,
Cup by cup, and stroke by stroke?

II

White as lilies, pure as candles,
Bowing modestly like stars,
From the heart's deep center shines,
With reddish rim, the glow of love.

Such premature narcissus
Bloom in rows within my garden.
May these kind ones know
Whom they're awaiting on their trellis.

III

When the sheep move from the meadow,
At once we see a green so pure;
But soon with motley flowers
It will bloom into a paradise.

Hope spreads its diaphanous veil
In misty shapes before our view:
Wish fulfillment, feast of sun,
Cloud-break, bring us happiness!

IV

The peacock's screech is ugly, but its cry
Reminds me of its paradise of plumage,
And so I do not find its screech repugnant.
With India's geese it's not at all the same,
To enjoy these birds is quite impossible:
They're ugly and their cry's beyond endurance.

V

Spread out the radiance of your joy
For the evening sun's gold beam,
Let your tail's wheel and wreath
Boast back at her with eyes of boldness.
She searches where there's verdant bloom
In gardens roofed with vaults of blue;
Where she sees a pair of lovers,
She knows she's found a wondrous thing.

VI

The cuckoo like the nightingale
Would love to make the spring its captive,
But everywhere already summer
Bursts with burs and thistles.
For me as well he's thickened
The light leafage on that tree,
Through which I stole the fairest glance
With eyes intent on love.
That painted roof's concealed from me,
The lattices and posts;
Where my peeping was my death,
There will be my Orient.

VII

From higher regions dusk descends,
What was near is now so far,
But first of all let it be raised–
The sweet light of the evening star!
All things waver indistinctly,
Mist ascends in creeping swirls,
And the lake at rest reflects
The deepened blackness of the night.

Now in regions to the east
I sense the moon's soft glow and warmth.
Slender willows' hair-like branches
Dally on the nearest waters.
Through the play of moving shadows
Trembles Luna's magic light,
And through the eye a coolness creeps,
Oozing peace into the heart.

VIII

She was fairer than the fairest day,
　　And so you must forgive me,
　　If I choose not to forget her,
　　　Especially not in nature.
She approached me in the garden,
　　To show me her good favor.
　　I feel it still and think of it
　　And stay devoted to her.

Always and Everywhere

Probe deeply in the shafts of mountains,
    Follow clouds through lofty air,
    Muses call to brook and valley,
    Beckoning a thousand times.

As soon as a fresh calyx blossoms,
    It demands new songs from you,
    And though time rush by and flee,
    Seasons always come again.

ANCIENT WORDS, ORPHIC

DAIMON, Ruling Spirit

As on the day which gave you to this world,
The sun assumed its place to greet the planets,
At once you flourished and continued thus to grow,
According to the law of your beginning.
So must you be- you cannot flee yourself,
As sibyls often said, as well as prophets,
And neither time nor might can break to pieces
A molded form, which through its life evolves.

TYCHE, Chance

And yet, these limits' strictures are surrounded
By a pleasing, shifting thing that changes with us;
You don't remain alone, you grow with others
And probably behave as others do.
In life things now fall for us, now against us,
It is a game and has to be played through;
And soon the years come quietly full circle,
The lamp awaits the flame that will ignite it.

EROS, Love

And it appears!- He falls down from the sky,
To which he flew from ancient, barren wastes,
Along the days of spring he glides on airy
Plumage, targeting your head and heart;
Seems first to flee, and then returns from flight,
To cause an anxious joy, a pain that's sweet.
So many hearts get lost in what is common,
But the noble are devoted to the One.

ANANGKE, Necessity

And then again it's as the stars decreed it:
Law and limitation; and all willing
Is simply wanting what we know we should,
And when this willing speaks our whims are silent;
What's dearest to the heart gets brushed away,
To hard necessity desire surrenders.
So, after many years of seeming free,
Our sphere becomes as small as when we started.

ELPIS, Hope

And yet, the stubborn portals of such limits
And impenetrable walls can be unlocked,
So let them stand as permanent as stone!
A light and lawless being stirs with life:
From layers of cloud, from fog and rain it lifts us,
As through its power we, too, develop pinions.
You've surely seen it, dreaming through all regions;
A flap of wings- and eons are behind us.

When, in the infinite, this sameness
Flows and recurs eternally,
And that vault of myriad aspect
Shuts powerfully, to join itself:
Then joy of life pours through all being,
The smallest and the greatest star;
And every surge, and every struggle
Is heavenly rest in God, the Lord.

Background note on the poem "Euphrosyne":

  This poem celebrates the memory of a promising young actress, Christiane Neumann-Becker, who under Goethe's tutelage graced the stage at the court theater in Weimar. While traveling through the Alps, Goethe received the sad news of her untimely death. The fiction he uses to transfigure this devastating experience only increases the emotional force of the subject, making the poem unique among expressions of loss. The title name is that of one of the three graces of mythology, but its literal meaning is, significantly, "joy."

Index of Poems
(by title or by opening words)

ISBN 142516922-8